That
Book
Woman

That Book Woman

HEATHER HENSON

pictures by DAVID SMALL

Atheneum Books for Young Readers

New York   London   Toronto   Sydney

My folks and me—
we live way up
as up can get.
So high
we hardly sight
a soul—
'cept hawks
a-winging in the sky
and critters
hid among the trees.

My name is Cal,
and I am not the first one
nor the least one neither.
But I am the oldest boy,
and I can help Pap
with the plowing
and I can fetch the sheep
when they take a-wander.

And I can bring the cow home too
come evening-time,
which is right handy,
seeing as how
my sister Lark
would keep her nose
a-twixt the pages of a book
daybreak to dusky dark
if Mama would allow.
The readenest child
you ever did see—
that's what Pap says.

Not me.
I was not born
to sit so stoney-still
a-staring at some chicken scratch.
And I do not fancy it one bit
when Lark plays Teacher—
the onliest school a jillion miles
back down the creek.
And even Lark can hardly
spread her wings and fly.
So now she aims
to school us herself.
But me, I am no scholar-boy.

That's why I am the first to hear
the clippitty-clop
and spy the sorrel mare—
red as clay.
I am the first to know
the rider is no man at all,
but a lady wearing britches
for all the world to see.

'Course we make that stranger
kindly welcome
and she's friendly as can be,
and after sips of sassy tea
she lays her saddlebag
upon the table
and what spills out
might just as well be
gold
the way Lark's eyes shine
penny-bright,
the way her hands
they won't keep still,
reaching out to grab
a treasure.

Now what that lady brings
it's sure no treasure,
not to me,
but books!
Would you believe?
A passel of books she's packed
clear up the mountainside!
A hard day's ride
and all for naught,
I reckon.
For if she aims to sell her wares
just like the tinker-man
who travels 'round
with pots and pans
and such,
it's but a plain and simple fact,
we have no greenbacks here,
no shiny coins to spend.
Least-ways not
on dumb old books.

Well, Pap he takes
one look at Lark
and clears his throat.
"A trade,"
he says.
"A poke of berries
for one book."
My hands double fist
behind my back.
I yearn to speak,
but daren't.
It is the very poke I picked—
for pie,
not books.

To my surprise
that lady shakes her head
real firm.
She will not take
a poke of berries
nor a mess of greens
nor any thing
Pap names to trade.
These books are free,
as free as air!
Not only that—
why, two weeks to the day
she'll come again
to swap these books
for more!

Now me,
I do not care one hoot
for what that Book Woman
has carried 'round,
and it would not bother me
at all
if she forgot the way
back to our door.
But here she'll come
right through the rain
and fog
and cold.

That horse of hers
sure must be brave,
I reckon.

Comes on a time
the world turns white
as Granpap's beard.
The wind it shrieks
like bobcats do
deep inside the dark of night.
So here we sit
tucked 'round the fire,
no thought to howdy-do's this day.
Why, even critters of the wild
will keep a-hid
come snow like this.

But sakes alive—
we hear a
tap tap tap
upon the window-glass.
And there she be—
wrapped tip to toe!
She makes her trade
right through the crack
to keep *us* folks
from catching cold.
And when Pap bids
her stay the night,
she only shakes her head.
"My horse will see me home,"
she says.

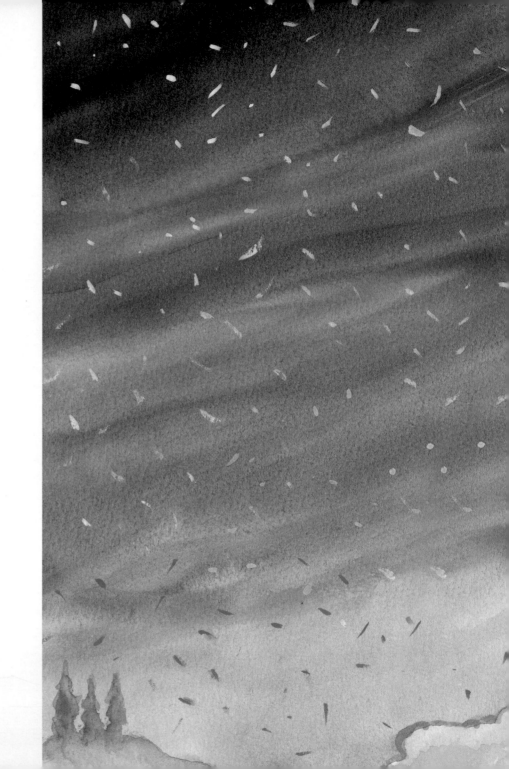

I stand a spell to watch
that Book Woman
disappear.
And thoughts
they go a-swirling 'round
inside my head,
just like the whirly-flakes
outside our door.
It's not the horse alone
that's brave,
I reckon,
but the rider, too.

And all at once
I yearn to know
what makes that Book Woman
risk catching cold,
or worse.

I pick a book with words
and pictures, too,
and hold it out.
"Teach me what it says."
And Lark,
she does not laugh
or even tease,
but makes a place,
and quiet-like,
we start to read.

Pap says it's written
in the signs
how long or short
the winter stays.
This year the signs
they all foretold
of deepest snow,
of cold eternal.
And even though
most days
we're tight as toes
pinched into boughten shoes,
I do not mind.
A puzzlement,
I know,
but true.

It's nigh on spring
before that Book Woman
can stop to visit a spell.
And Mama makes a gift—
the only precious thing she can—
her recipe for berry pie,
which is the best grub earthly.
"Not much, I know,
for all your trouble,"
Mama says,
and then her voice
goes low with pride,
"and for making
two readers outta one."

I duck my head
and wait until the very last
to speak my mind:
"Wish there was something
I could gift you too."
That Book Woman
turns to look at me
with big dark eyes.
"Come here, Cal,"
she says real gentle,
and I come close.
"Read me something."

I open up the book I'm holding,
a new one brought
this very day.
Just chicken scratch,
I used to figure,
but now I see
what's truly there,
and I read a little out.

"That's gift enough,"
she says,
and smiles so big,
it makes me smile
right back.

Author's Note

This story was inspired by the true and courageous work of the Pack Horse Librarians, who were known as "Book Women" in the Appalachian Mountains of Kentucky.

The Pack Horse Library Project was founded in the 1930s as part of President Franklin D. Roosevelt's Works Progress Administration in order to bring books to remote regions where there were few schools and no libraries. High in the hills of Kentucky, roads were often just creek beds or rough trails. A Book Woman would travel, by horse or by mule, the same arduous route every two weeks, carrying a load of books—in good weather and in bad. To show their gratitude for what came "free as air," a family might make a gift from what little they had: garden vegetables, wildflowers, berries, or cherished recipes passed down through generations.

While there were a few men among the Pack Horse Librarians, the jobs were mainly filled by women, in a time when most people felt that "a woman's work was in the home." The Book Women were remarkable in their resilience and their dedication. They were paid very little, but they were proud of what they did: bringing the outside world to the people of Appalachia, and sometimes making readers out of those who had never seen much use for "chicken scratch."

In Kentucky, creek beds and trails eventually became roads. Horses and mules gave way to the kind of Bookmobiles that still exist today. All across the country, dedicated librarians continue to bring books to folks who need them.

The following resources will help you learn more about the kind of Book Woman portrayed in these pages:

Websites:
Kentucky Department for Libraries and Archives: http://www.kdla.ky.gov
New Deal Network: http://newdeal.feri.org
Franklin D. Roosevelt Library and Museum: http://www.fdrlibrary.marist.gov

Books:
Appelt, Kathi, and Jeanne Cannella Schmitzer. *Down Cut Shin Creek: The Pack Horse Librarians of Kentucky.* New York: HarperCollins, 2001.
Caudill, Harry M. *Night Comes to the Cumberlands: A Biography of a Depressed Area.* Boston: Little, Brown and Company, 1963.

For my mother, my very first book woman
—H. H.

For Sarah, my book woman
—D. S.

Atheneum Books for Young Readers ≈ An imprint of Simon & Schuster Children's Publishing Division ≈ 1230 Avenue of the Americas, New York, New York 10020 ≈ Text copyright © 2008 by Heather Henson ≈ Illustrations copyright © 2008 by David Small ≈ All rights reserved, including the right of reproduction in whole or in part in any form. ≈ Book design by Dan Potash ≈ The text for this book is set in Grit Primer. ≈ The illustrations for this book are rendered in ink, watercolor, and pastel chalk. ≈ Manufactured in China ≈ 0715 SCP ≈ 10   ≈ Library of Congress Cataloging-in-Publication Data ≈ Henson, Heather. ≈ That Book Woman / Heather Henson ; illustrated by David Small. —1st ed. ≈ p. cm. ≈ Summary: A family living in the Appalachian Mountains in the 1930s gets books to read during the regular visits of the "Book Woman"—a librarian who rides a pack horse through the mountains, lending books to the isolated residents. ≈ ISBN-13: 978-1-4169-0812-8 ≈ ISBN-10: 1-4169-0812-9 ≈ [1. Books and reading—Fiction. 2. Librarians—Fiction. 3. Appalachian Region—History—20th century—Fiction.] I. Small, David, 1945– ill. II. Title. III. Title: That Book Woman. ≈ PZ7.H39863Th 2008 ≈ [E]—dc22 ≈ 2007018156